GETTING OUR KIDS FROM PLAYTIME TO BEDTIME IS NO EASY TASK.

THIS BOOK IS MEANT TO BE READ TO YOUR KIDDOS AS A FUN-FILLED GUIDE TO TRICKING THEM INTO GOING FROM PLAYTIME TO BEDTIME!

...OOPS, WAIT DON'T READ THEM THIS PART.

ENJOY!

DEDICATED TO MY
SPECIAL READER
&
OUR LITTLE/TALL MONSTERS

PlaytimeSeries.com

ISBN 979-8-3607490-9-7 (Paperback)
ISBN 979-8-9871675-2-6 (Hardcover)
ISBN 979-8-9871675-0-2 (eBook)

First Edition

IT'S BEDTIME NOT PLAYTIME

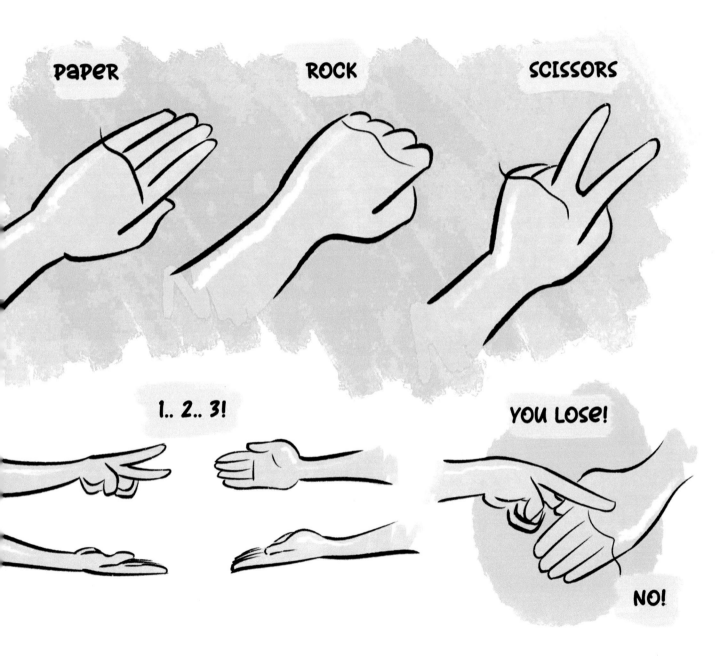

STEP 1: BATH & PAJAMAS

STEP 3: BRUSH & POTTY

ONLY A DOT OF TOOTHPASTE IS NEEDED.

NOT A BIG GLOB OF TOOTHPASTE.

SET A TWO MINUTE TIMER.

BRUSHING IN CIRCLES IS BETTER. INSTEAD OF BACK AND FORTH.

DON'T FORGET TO BRUSH YOUR GERMY TONGUE!

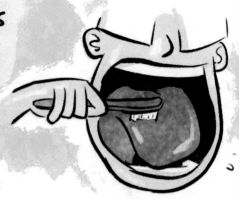

WE'RE DOING GREAT, KIDDOS! THREE STEPS ARE DONE.
REMEMBER THE NEXT STEP?
OF COURSE WE DO!

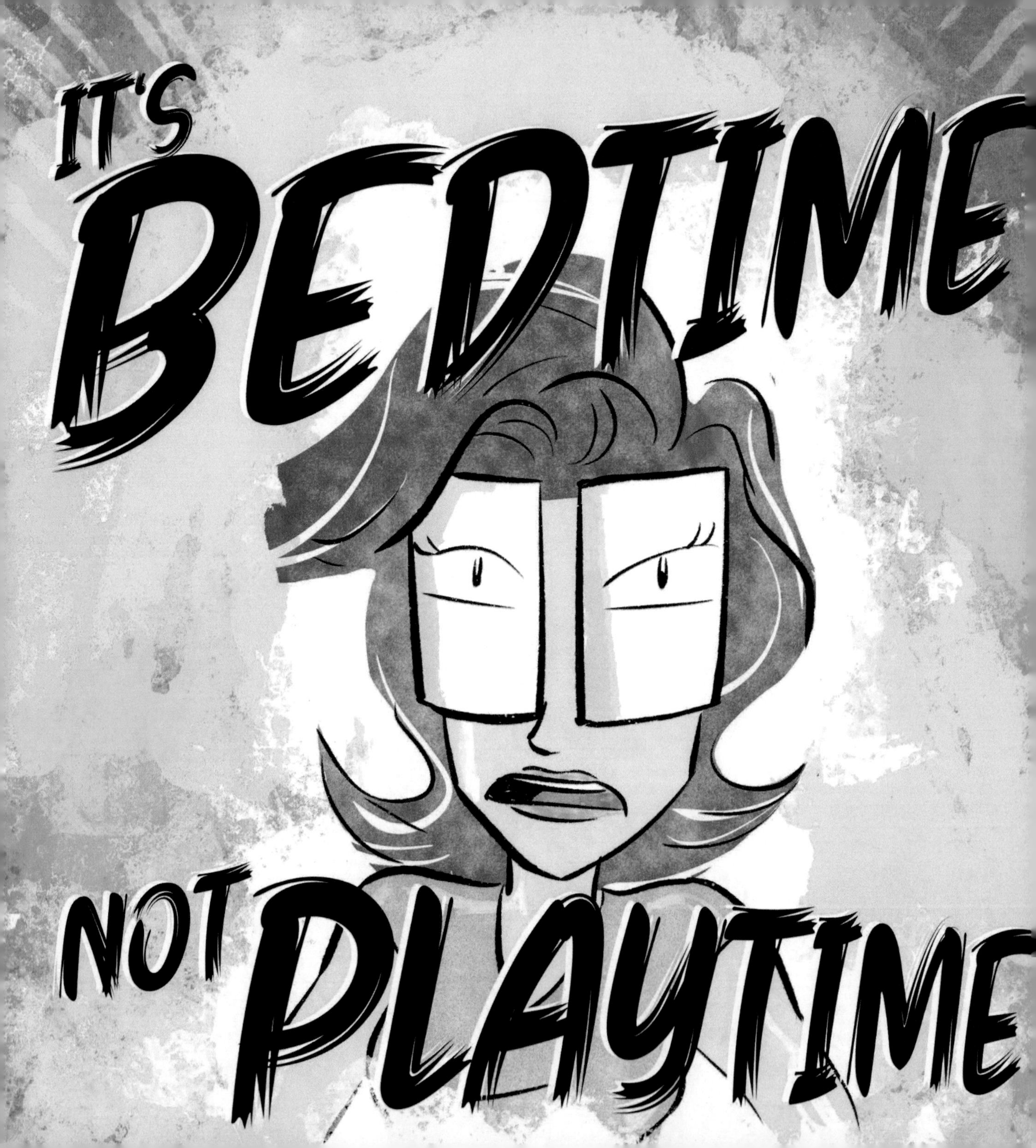
IT'S BEDTIME
NOT PLAYTIME

STEP 4: HUGS & KISSES

...WHERE I CAN REST.

It's
BEDTIME
NOT
PLAYTIME

PlaytimeSeries.com

About The ~~Author~~ KIDS

C. Santiago started drawing when he was 8 years old...

Blah, blah, blah! Enough about our parents. You all wanna know about us, the real stars of the book. Avoiding bedtime is our super power! If it wasn't for us driving our parents crazy, you wouldn't be reading this. Wait a minute, how much are we getting paid for this?

Mom! Dad! Where's our Ferrari!?

Made in the USA
Las Vegas, NV
13 January 2024

84268417R00024